# I'm Reading About

# The U.S. CONSTITUTION

GALLOPADE

by Carole Marsh

Printed and Manufactured in Peachtree City, GA., USA www.gallopade.com
Book design: Susan Van Denhende
Editor: Janice Baker



Photo Credits: Cover: danielfela/Bigstock.com. Page 3: Lisann23/Bigstock.com. Page 5A: Dougbraphael/Bigstock.com; 5B: www.whitehouse.gov; 5C: holbox/Bigstock.com. Page 7: PromesaArtStudio/Bigstock.com; 7A: Asher B. Durand, U.S. Navy; 7B: National Portrait Gallery, Washington, D.C.; 7C: The White House Historical Association; 7D: Gilbert Stuart, Clark Art Institute. Page 9: Howard Chandler Christy, United States House of Representatives. Pages 5, 11, 28: flippo/Bigstock.com. Page 13A: p.lange/Bigstock.com; 13B: Michael Darcy Brown/ Bigstock.com. Page 17: AndreyPopov/Bigstock.com. Page 20: Library of Congress. Page 22: Gramper/Bigstock.com. Page 24: Ken Lund, CC BY-SA 2.0. Page 26: U.S. Department of State. Page 28 (All Bigstock.com) 28A: lightpoet; 28B: Anna Nahabed; 28C: Kasia Bialasiewicz; 28D: kiankhoon; 28E: Inked Pixels. Page 30 (All Bigstock.com) klikk; 30A: dmstudio; 30B: ginasanders; 30C: Andreyuu. Page 32: Zerbor/Bigstock.com. Page 34A: Orhan/Bigstock.com; 34B: U.S. Army.

The U.S. Constitution is the supreme law of the United States!

What is so special about the Constitution?

Let's read about it and see!

# INTRODUCTION

The Constitution of the United States
is a very important document.
It is a set of rules that Americans must live by.

The Constitution set up America's government.
It created the President of the United States.
It created Congress and the Supreme Court!

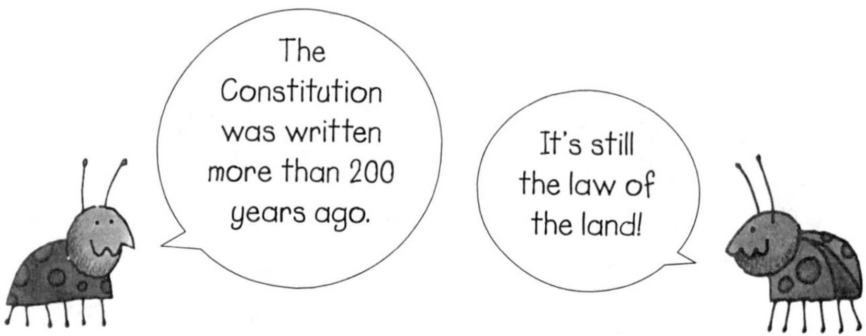

# America's Government

Supreme Court

President

Congress

HISTORY

The first written plan for U.S. government
was the Articles of Confederation.
But it left the government too weak to
meet the country's needs.

In 1787, a group of men met in Philadelphia, Pennsylvania.
They wanted to write a new set of laws
for the United States of America.
Their meeting was called the "Constitutional Convention."

Those men were the "Framers of the Constitution."

# Famous Framers

MADISON

James Madison had many ideas
for the new government.
He had written Virginia's Constitution
years before, so he had experience!

James Madison wanted America to have
a strong central government.
He also wanted to make sure that
all Americans kept their rights and freedoms!

He is known as the "Father of the Constitution."

# Creating the Constitution

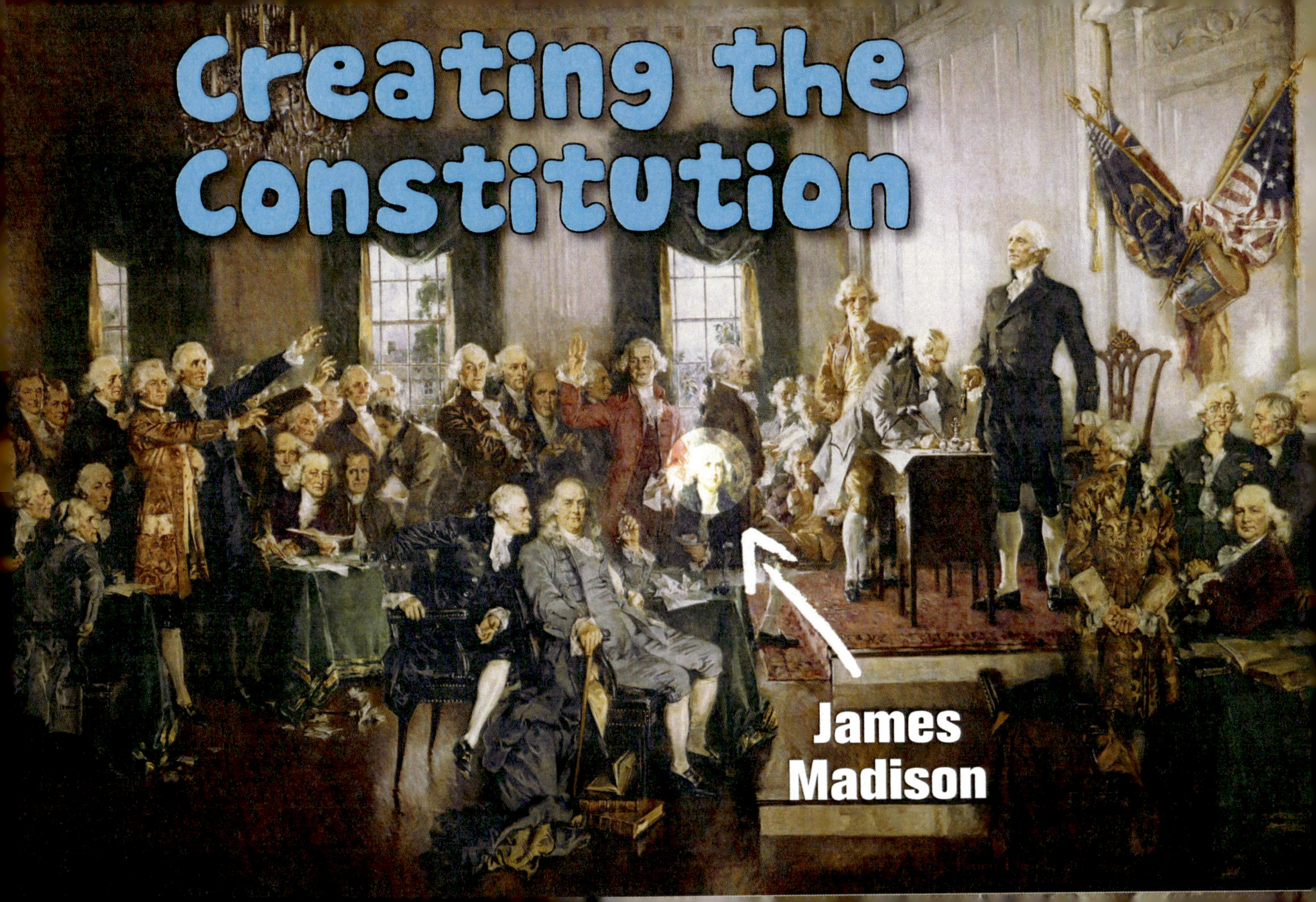

# PREAMBLE

The first paragraph of the Constitution
is called the "Preamble."
It explains the purpose of the Constitution.

The Preamble to the U.S. Constitution begins
with the words: "We the People."
Those words make clear that the government's power
comes from the people!

When the people have power, they can make changes
to the government and elect new leaders.

# Preamble

We the People
insure domestic Tranquility, provide for the common
and our Posterity, do ordain and establish this Constit
Article. I

# FEDERALISM

The Constitution set up a federal system
of government.
In a federal system, power is shared between
the national government and the state governments.

The states take care of their own affairs,
like schools and local elections.
The national government handles things that
affect the whole country, like the military.

The national government is also
known as the "federal government."

# Federal System

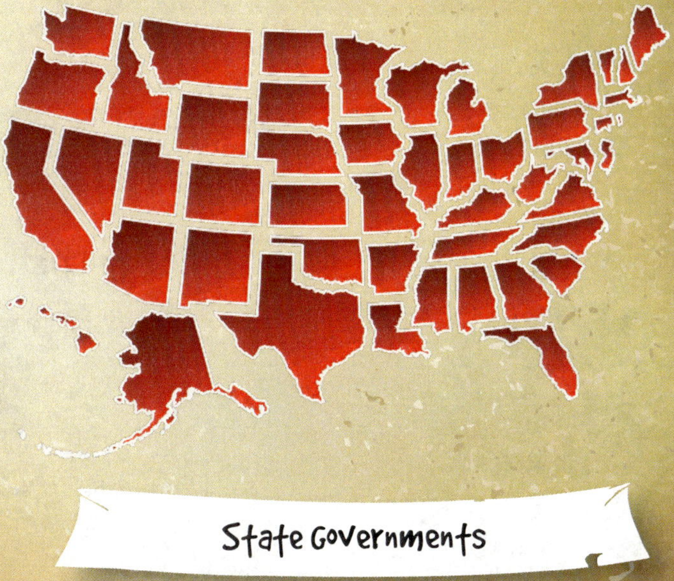

# BRANCHES

The Constitution divides our government into three branches:

- The **Legislative Branch** is headed by Congress. It creates and passes laws.
- The **Executive Branch** is headed by the President. It carries out and enforces laws.
- The **Judicial Branch** is headed by the Supreme Court. It interprets and applies the laws.

**The Judicial Branch makes sure that laws agree with the Constitution.**

# Three Branches

## Executive Branch

The president carries out the laws.

## Legislative Branch

Congress makes the laws.

## Judicial Branch

Courts will settle legal arguments.

## POWER

The Constitution says that no branch of government has more power than the other branches. Each branch has ways to check the power of the other two branches.

This system is called "checks and balances." Checks and balances make sure that power is shared. That protects the American people!

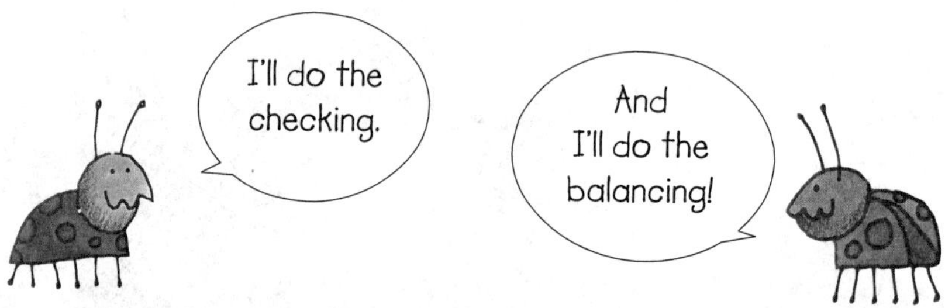

# Checks and Balances

Congress
Senate:
equal representation
House of Representatives:
based on population
Great Compromise

REPRESENTATION

The Framers of the Constitution did not agree on everything. They had to compromise!

One issue was how states would be represented in Congress. Small states thought the big states would overpower them! The Framers compromised by having two houses in Congress. This became known as the "Great Compromise."

- **Senate:** each state has an equal number of representatives
- **House of Representatives:** each state is represented according to its population

# Compromise over Slavery

SLAVERY

Another issue facing the Framers was slavery.
There were a lot of slaves in the Southern states.

Delegates from the Southern states wanted slaves counted as part of their population.
That way, they got more members in Congress.
Delegates from Northern states said NO!

Finally, a compromise was reached.
Delegates decided to let Southern states count their free population plus 3/5 of their slave population.

# Amendments

# CHANGES

The Framers of the Constitution were very wise. They realized that the Constitution might need to be changed in the future.

The Framers added a process to make changes. The Constitution can be changed by an "amendment." Congress proposes amendments, and the states have to approve them.

There have been 27 amendments to the U.S. Constitution.

# Ratify the Constitution

By September 1787, delegates to the convention had finished writing the Constitution. But the work was not complete!

What was the next step? The states had to ratify, or approve, the Constitution.

By 1789, 9 of the 13 states had ratified the document. That was the magic number of states needed to make the Constitution the law of the land!

The final state, Rhode Island, ratified it in 1790.

## RATIFY

# Bill of Rights

# BILL OF RIGHTS

Some delegates had a problem ratifying the Constitution.
They wanted it to have a "Bill of Rights."
Americans had just fought a war for independence.
Their new rights needed to be protected!

James Madison agreed, and wrote 12 amendments.
He clearly listed certain rights and freedoms.
Ten of those amendments were passed.
They are known as the "Bill of Rights."

In 1808, James Madison was elected the 4th President of the United States.

# First Amendment

FIRST AMENDMENT

The First Amendment is the most well-known amendment in the Bill of Rights.
It protects many important rights and freedoms:

- Right to speak freely
- Right to practice your religion
- Right to meet together peacefully
- Right to petition the government
- Freedom of the press

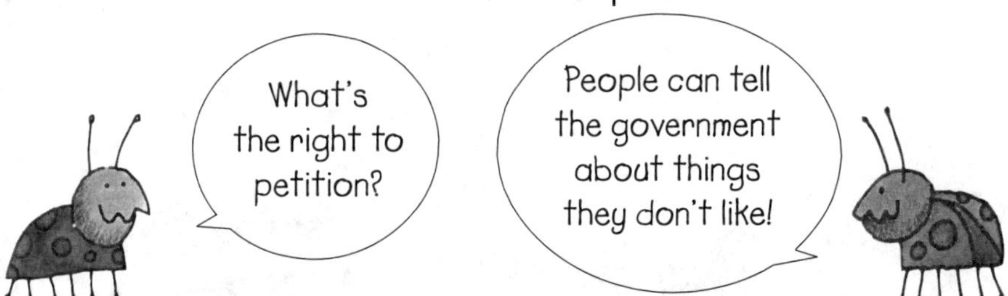

# More Amendments

Fairness

Freedom

Right to Vote

All of the amendments to the Constitution are important. But some of them have made a very big impact on American life:

- 6th Amendment: Citizens have the right to a fair trial
- 13th Amendment: Slavery abolished
- 15th Amendment: Black men given the right to vote
- 19th Amendment: Women given the right to vote
- 26th Amendment: Voting age set to 18 years

Constitution
Incredible Constitution

# DID YOU KNOW?

Read these fascinating facts about the Constitution!

- The U.S. Constitution has about 4,500 words.
- It took about 100 days to complete the Constitution.
- The last amendment was added in 1992.
- Benjamin Franklin (81) was the oldest man to sign it.
- The U.S. Constitution is the longest-lasting constitution of any government in the world!

# National Archives

You can see the original U.S. Constitution at the National Archives in Washington, D.C.

All four pages of the Constitution lie in a display case protected by special glass. The case is kept at a specific temperature and humidity level to preserve the paper.

The U.S. Constitution guarantees the rights and freedoms of all Americans!

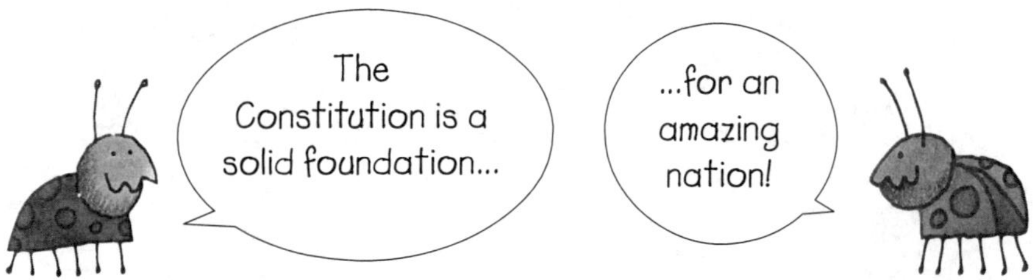


ORIGINAL

# GLOSSARY

**abolish:** to do away with

**compromise:** to give up some of your demands to reach an agreement

**convention:** a meeting of people for a common purpose

**delegate:** a person sent to a conference to represent others

**enforce:** to make sure people do what is required by law

**foundation:** an underlying basis or principle for something

**interpret:** to explain the meaning of something

**ratify:** to make an agreement official by signing it or voting for it